YA KNU
Knudsen, Shannon
Rise above

RISE ABOVE

THE RED ZONE

RISE ABOVE

SHANNON KNUDSEN

MINNEAPOLIS

Darby Creek
A division of Lerner Publishing Group, Inc.
241 First Avenue North
Minneapolis, MN 55401 USA

For reading levels and more information, look up this title at www.lernerbooks.com.

Front cover © Mike Powell/CORBIS. Backgrounds: © iStockphoto.com/mack2happy, (grass).

Main body text set in Janson Text LT Std 12/17.
Typeface provided by Linotype AG.

Library of Congress Cataloging-in-Publication Data

Knudsen, Shannon, 1971–
    Rise above / by Shannon Knudsen.
        pages cm. — (The red zone ; #6)
    Summary: "One of the Trojans' assistant coaches is giving a few players special attention. That includes a (maybe illegal) personal nutrition program. Will the players go along in order to get an edge?"— Provided by publisher.
    ISBN 978–1–4677–2127–1 (lib. bdg. : alk. paper)
    ISBN 978–1–4677–4654–0 (eBook)
    [1. Football—Fiction. 2. Steroids—Fiction. 3. High schools—Fiction. 4. Schools—Fiction.] I. Title.
PZ7.K78355Ri 2014
[Fic]—dc23   2014000751

Manufactured in the United States of America
1 – SB – 7/15/14

FOR MY FAVORITE FOOTBALL FAN,
BRENDA BAREFIELD

1/FRIDAY, NOVEMBER 15—
PRACTICE, SEVEN DAYS
BEFORE STATE PLAYOFFS

When you run the forty-yard dash, you can't tell how fast you're going. You're too busy working your legs, pounding the turf, and pumping your arms to give a thought to the stopwatch in Coach Kramer's hand. You know if it feels good—like, *yeah*, I got this—and you know if it doesn't. But you never know until you cross the line if the number Coach calls out will be your record or just another piece of data for his clipboard.

Not usually.

"Four-eight-six!" Coach Kramer hollered as I flashed by. Might not turn a scout's head, but for me? Sweet.

I eased up and circled back around in time to see the man's face crack into his signature grin, the one he only lets out if you've made his day. "Another personal best for Burns!"

The guys on the sideline—the small group Coach Kramer had assembled for today's extra workout—gave me high fives as I jogged past them. Well, most of them did. Ian McNamara looked the other way, like something truly fascinating was going on downfield.

"Awright, Red Hot!" Fullback Dylan Davis punched me in the arm. "You keep this up, I'll be blocking for you in the playoffs."

I hadn't been Red Hot Burns until a week ago. All season long, I was just plain old Darius. But then it happened. First came my personal best on the bench press—not just weight, reps too. Leg press, same thing. When I started smoking the forty, people started to pay attention. Throw in a couple stellar runs in our last game, and I had myself a new nickname.

Now I'd done it again—broken my own record in the forty. The same record I'd set just a week before. Dylan was right. I was on fire, and everybody knew it.

Ian snorted. "Red Hot? Try Roid Hot." Coach was too far away to hear him, but everyone else did.

Half a second later, Terry Foster was up in his face, pointing a finger. "No way," he hissed. "No way, Ian. You do not go there. Not now, not ever."

Huh. Who would have thought it? Terry had never said two words to me, yet here he was standing up for second-stringer Darius Burns. But when I thought about it, I realized he was just standing up for himself. After all, we were all in this together. And we all knew how dangerous it would be to say certain words out loud.

Ian had his reasons to be mad, though. He and I had a serious rivalry going on over the starting halfback slot. Devon Shaw had pretty much owned the position all season. But last week, Devon had surgery on his wrist for a torn ligament. That left a serious gap in the Trojan starting lineup as we prepped for the state play-offs. It was a gap I intended to fill. So did Ian.

"You just keep trying, McNamara," I told him. "Keep trying."

He glared at me, but I laughed it off. Truth was, either of us could end up starting in the playoffs. The guys hadn't started calling me Red Hot for nothing, but Ian had speed, agility, and size, a combination I couldn't challenge just by practicing my sprints or pumping iron.

Don't get me wrong, I had plenty to offer the team. I had guts, I had toughness, and I could handle the ball like nobody's business. Plus I knew the playbook backwards, forwards, and upside down.

But when it came to finding the hole at crunch time, on a field full of guys looking for someone to smash? There, Ian could make plays. I might be the one racking up the numbers for now. And yeah, Coach Kramer couldn't be happier with me. But Coach Zachary—our head coach, the only guy I truly needed to impress—couldn't care less about nicknames or even records. When it came time to line up, he would go with the guy who could get the job done.

I wanted it to be me. I *needed* it to be me. And if that meant I had to do whatever it took to get an extra edge, well, that's what I'd do.

Of course, so would Ian McNamara.

2/FRIDAY, NOVEMBER 15—
AT HOME

Dinner that night was late. My parents run a law firm—Burns and Caldwell-Burns, Attorneys at Law—so we eat a lot of takeout food. Tonight's special? Chinese, complete with egg rolls. I grabbed four and piled a bunch of moo goo gai pan onto fried rice.

As we sat down, my little sister claimed center stage. "Oh, my gosh! Mama, Daddy, you will not believe what happened today. You know that kid, Jeremy Bolger? Well, he brought firecrackers on the bus. Hid them in his backpack, and then when the bus hit a big pothole . . ."

Monique's OK, but, man, that girl can talk. I splashed some soy sauce on my food and settled in for a detailed description of the latest seventh-grade drama.

Three egg rolls later, she was still going on. I tilted back in my chair and stabbed at some snow peas with my fork. I couldn't stop thinking about Ian's stupid comment at practice. Roid Hot? Ian was juicing too. Where did he get off giving me grief about it? As far as I could tell, the only thing he had to be upset about was the fact that I was seeing way more benefits than he was.

Crash! The chair slid out from under me. My fork clattered to the floor, snow peas still attached. I ended up on my butt.

Very smooth, Darius.

Monique laughed so hard she almost spit out her cashew chicken.

"Darius!" Mama said. "How many times do I have to tell you?" And off she went about table manners and proper posture and I don't know what else. I pushed myself off the floor and started looking for my missing dignity, which was nowhere to be found.

"Sorry, Mama," I said when I could get a word in edgewise. "Um, may I be excused to do my homework?" She nodded, and I put my chair back in its place—very quietly—and took my plate to the sink and rinsed it off.

"Darius," Mama said, "before you go, tell us how that biology quiz turned out." She raised her eyebrows like she always does when she means business.

"Yeah," Dad chimed in. "Are we going to need to get you a tutor?"

I groaned. Biology is my worst subject. I'm pulling a B minus, which you'd think would be good enough for most parents. Especially considering that football is practically a full-time job. But it's not good enough for Princeton University, which means it's not good enough for Marcus Burns—and definitely not for Sheila Caldwell-Burns. They've got my whole future mapped out, and it does not include any B minuses.

Mama and Dad met at Princeton. Dad's father, my Grandpa Burns, went there too. Ever since I was in first grade, all three of them have been telling me how great it'll be when I make it three generations of Burnses attending the world's finest university. Once it started looking like I had a chance in football, Mama added an athletic scholarship to the big dream.

I'm not arrogant enough to think I'd ever get a scholarship to a real football school like Ohio State, but the Ivy League? That might actually happen—if I keep my grades sky-high, do some community service, and throw in a couple other extracurriculars during the off-season.

No pressure here at all. Nope.

"Well?" Mama asked. "We're waiting."

"B plus," I said, studying the pattern of the tile squares on the kitchen floor.

"Hmm," Dad said. "A step in the right direction. Good job, Son."

I waited for Mama's verdict. She just nodded, which meant that she wasn't thrilled but wouldn't pull the trigger on tutoring just yet.

Twenty minutes later, I had my laptop and

my biology textbook out on my desk, but photosynthesis was the last thing on my mind. I had to admit it: Even though I'd brushed McNamara off at practice, his words had hit their mark. *Roid Hot.* Yeah, that was me.

My eyes wandered to the photo on my desk, an autographed picture of Marion Motley that my dad had found on eBay. Motley's kind of my hero, even though he played fullback, not halfback. He was one of the guys who broke the color barrier in the NFL back in 1946, playing for the Cleveland Browns. But he did a lot more than that. He made the Hall of Fame—and he did it on his own merits during a time when the odds were stacked against him.

Ping! My cell phone brought me back to the present. It was a text from Curtis Benson, one of our free safeties and my best friend. *Yo D. Pizza?*

Already ate, I typed back.

So what. Live a little, man. Have dessert.

Gotta study.

The phone rang. Looked like Curtis wasn't letting me off that easy.

"Dude," I said as I answered the phone. "If

I don't ace the next biology test, my parents are gonna make me get a tutor."

"Darius, listen, I gotta talk to you. Just come out for an hour."

Curtis never sounded that serious.

"Pick me up in ten," I said.

3/FRIDAY, NOVEMBER 15—
DOYLE'S PIZZA

Curtis drove to Doyle's, the team's favorite hangout. Decent pizza—and all you can eat for free if you're one of the Big Six, the offensive playmakers. Which meant I paid for every slice.

But if I beat out McNamara for Devon's slot at halfback? Oh, yeah. That'd put me in the Big Six for sure.

A punch in the arm shook me out of my daydream. Curtis was acting like usual, but I knew he was rattled about something when he steered away from the other guys, picking a booth in the shadows at the back of the restaurant instead.

"So what's the big emergency?" I asked, slurping my soda.

"You are," he said. He looked like somebody had died or something.

"Say what?"

Curtis shook his head. "Don't BS me, Darius. Something's different with you, and I wanna know what it is."

I was in mid-slurp as he spoke, and I swallowed the wrong way, sending soda down my windpipe. I coughed and hacked for a few seconds longer than I really needed to. "Dang, I hate that feeling. Tickles."

Curtis crossed his arms and stared me down.

Did he know? How? Had someone talked? And what was I supposed to say now? I'd never lied to Curtis, but there was no way I could tell him the truth.

I tried to lighten the mood. "Dude, your pizza's getting cold."

"Screw the pizza," he said. "Come on, man.

I saw you run for Coach Kramer today. At your Elite Whatevers practice."

"Warriors. Elite Warriors."

"Like I said, Elite Whatevers."

I scrambled for time. "You were there? Where? I didn't see you."

"What's it matter where I was? Point is, I've known you for ten years. I've played football with you since Half Backs camp. You ain't that fast, Darius." Curtis still hadn't taken a bite of his food.

"I am now." I glared at him. "You saw it yourself."

"Yeah, but why now? Why all of a sudden? How come you can press forty pounds more than you could at the beginning of the season?"

"How should I know? It's probably a growth spurt. You know, some guys come into their own at our age. It happens."

He looked up at the ceiling, then back at me, eyes narrowed. "Don't talk to me like I'm some kind of idiot."

"Why not? You're acting like one." I stood up from the table. "You have something to say, just say it."

Curtis sighed. "Sit down, man." I stood my ground. "Awright, D. I know what I'm talking about here. And you know what I'm talking about. But you wanna pretend you don't, fine."

"I'm not pretending." The words came out flat, without conviction.

Curtis shook his head. "You know, you think you know a guy through and through . . ." He trailed off.

"You do know me, Curtis. I'm the same guy I always was."

"Naw, you ain't. I never had you pegged for a cheater."

I stood there with my mouth open.

"Just listen, man. You gotta—I don't know. You gotta be careful, y'know what I'm sayin'? You gotta watch your back. And make sure you don't get hurt."

"I have no idea what you're talking about," I said.

"Just take care of yourself."

"I'm fine, Curtis. Everything's fine." I started walking away.

"Naw, it ain't."

I kept walking. He didn't come after me.

Ditching Curtis left me with no ride home, just a two-mile walk in chilly November air. At least the walk gave me plenty of time to try to make myself feel better about lying to my best friend.

He doesn't need to know, I told myself. He's meddling where he's not needed. And he's probably just guessing, just jealous of how far I've come this season. There's no way I'm about to jeopardize everything I've worked for. There's no way I'll risk getting Coach Kramer in trouble or the other guys in the Elite. Or myself, for that matter.

It was a pretty good speech I gave myself. But it didn't work. I guess my BS detector is too sharp for my own good sometimes.

How did I get myself into this?

4/EIGHT WEEKS EARLIER

It had started eight weeks ago. We'd lost to the Carroll Cyclones the night before, and Coach Z just about went into cardiac arrest chewing us out in the locker room the next day. "Show me a good loser!" he yelled, going into Vince Lombardi mode for the millionth time. "Show me a good loser, and I'll show you a *loser*!"

Practice was brutal that day. We ran laps. We ran the stairs. We ran suicides. We hit the sleds and dummies for extra reps. At least four guys puked. I felt lucky I wasn't one of them.

After Coach Z dismissed us, we staggered around like drunken fools, trying to catch our breath. That's when Coach Kramer, who doubles as special teams coach and assistant offensive coach, tapped me on the shoulder.

"Other end of the field, Burns," he said. I couldn't believe my ears. He wanted *more* out of us?

"But Coach Z said—" That earned me quite the look. I hustled downfield—if you can call a slow jog hustling.

But most of the team didn't follow. Turned out Coach Kramer only wanted some of the team's "most dependable" starting offensive backs and a few backups. Including me.

He began with a Speech, the kind that deserves a capital letter because it sounds so serious and important. Like when the president goes on TV to announce that we're bombing another country.

"Some of you are this team's playmakers," he said. "And some of you are the playmakers of the very near future."

I knew which group I was in, of course. Devon hadn't hurt his wrist yet at that point, so I was—at best—a playmaker of the future.

Coach kept talking. "All of you have been identified as players with stellar potential. The kind of potential that can ensure we don't have more losses like Friday's or more practices like today's. You gentlemen are this team's hope. You are its elite. And from today on, you will be challenged to carry that mantle with an intensity you've never exhibited before."

Now that's how you get a bunch of football players' attention. Coach Kramer laid out the plan: extra workouts, extra game film, and individualized training for all of us, starting the next day. We were his Elite Trojan Warriors, he said. He made sure we understood that Coach Z and Coach Whitson, the head offensive coach, had approved the Warriors program. And he assured us that he would be on us constantly, pushing us to exceed our potential.

And at first, that's exactly how it was. Lots of skills coaching, extra time in the weight room, and studying film, that kind of thing. It was pretty sweet, working out with the first string, feeling like I was on the edge of being one of them. Then, the second week, Coach Kramer changed things up.

"New regimen," he announced at the end of a skills session. "Everyone line up." He passed out photocopied pages. "This is a high-protein diet, gentlemen. Nothing crazy, just some guidelines to help you bulk up. Start this program immediately. Along with the diet, you'll receive nutritional supplements." And with that, he started passing out water bottles and a couple of pills for each of us.

Even back then, something about it smelled funny. Like, if it was vitamins, wouldn't Coach just hand out a bottle to everybody and tell us to take it with dinner or whatever? And then there was his face. He was smiling too hard. That freaky grin. So, yeah, I wondered.

Anyone who's not a complete moron knows that steroids can mess you up. But when you play football, you learn on day one that when a coach says jump, not only do you ask how high, you ask how far and whether it's okay to land when you're done. What Coach Z says goes. And if Coach Z isn't around, you respond to his assistant coaches just like you'd respond to him.

Maybe that's why I didn't ask any questions. I figured, no way would a coach give me something that's not okay. Right? He says it's vitamins, that's good enough for me.

I was last in line. "Down the hatch, Burns," Coach Kramer said.

The pills looked like candy—little pink tablets with five sides. I popped them and took a slug of water. Coach was still showing that big wolf grin, like we were getting away with something clever.

"Listen up," he told us. "Every day after team practice, this group will stay behind to get your supplements. Now, I'd give these things to the whole team if I could, but they're expensive. So we keep this to ourselves. Is that understood?"

"Yes, sir!" we responded, just like we'd all been taught.

"Hands in!" We circled and extended our arms to the middle, palms facing down.

"Who are you?" Coach Kramer thundered.

"We! Are! Elite!" we yelled, pumping our arms at each word.

Coach set up an efficient system. One dose each day after practice or right before kickoff on Fridays. Even on Sundays, he pulled the Elite Warriors together for an hour of drills followed by supplements. After the first couple weeks, he swapped the pills for injections. He just pulled a bunch of syringes and a vial out of his black gym bag, casual as could be, and told us to line up.

Nobody said a word. Including me. And that's how I became, in the words of my best friend, a cheater.

5/MONDAY, NOVEMBER 18—
TEAM PRACTICE

Next day at practice, Coach Z had us run
through a bunch of plays. He told us we'd run
the same pattern four times, twice with me
in and twice with McNamara. It was obvious
what he had in mind. He wanted to see how we
stacked up against each other.

First came blasts. Coach gave us a scenario:
third and one. My job was to take the handoff
from Shane Hunter, our QB1. I'd find the hole

Dylan made ahead of me and dive through for enough yardage to make first down. Sounds simple enough, right? Sure it is, if you're at home watching it happen on TV. Out on the field, with guys coming at you from every direction, it's another story. You aim for the hole, lower your head, and try to move the pile before the pile obliterates you.

The main reason I'm not crazy about blasts is that I'm on the smaller side for a halfback. Sprinting is my game, dodging and dancing on the open field, not in a big pile. It's a critical skill, though, so I'd been pushing hard on it. And that day, I converted on both tries.

Ian had a couple of inches on me, plus maybe twenty pounds, so he excelled at punching through holes to pick up a yard or two. It came as no surprise that he made both his first downs too.

Next, we ran counters and reverses. McNamara made an impression, but so did I. My footwork was maybe a little faster than Ian's, but I couldn't tell what Coach Z was thinking. Unless that man is screaming or quoting Vince Lombardi, he's pretty hard to read.

When it came time to run pitches, I nailed it again, both times. But when Ian's turn came, it didn't go so well. He caught the pitch from Shane just fine, but as he dashed for the hole, the ball popped right out of his arms. Nobody had even hit him. He just fumbled without cause. He fell right on the ball, but the damage was done.

Coach blew the whistle, but before Ian could even get up, Terry Foster was all over him.

"You idiot!" he yelled, bending over Ian and yelling right in his face. "You think your job is to give away the ball? You think it's Christmastime for the Clinton Tigers and you're Santa Claus?"

"Jeez, man. Chill," McNamara said. He scrambled up, giving Terry a shoulder bump as he got to his feet.

Terry responded with a push. Ian said something too low for the rest of us to hear, and then Terry hauled back like he was about to punch him.

"You wanna see roid rage?" Terry yelled. "I'll show you some roid rage, you moron."

Coach Kramer got between them then, probably just in time to prevent a serious fight. I'd seen Terry get bent out of shape before but never like this. Not over something as minor as a fumble in a practice. He really looked like he wanted to pound Ian into the ground.

Coach Z had no patience for that kind of garbage. He sent us all to run laps. As I jogged, I thought about the exchange. Ian must have said something to Terry about roid rage.

It was pretty weird—Terry yelling about the treatments in front of the whole team. Just a couple days ago, he'd bitten Ian's head off for calling me Roid Hot at Elite Warriors. What was going on with him?

I'd heard of roid rage before, but I figured it was some kind of myth. One of those things doctors come up with to scare people away from doping. Now I had to wonder. What if it wasn't?

I needed some answers. Not from Coach Kramer, not from Curtis, and definitely not from my parents. I needed to do my own research.

6/TUESDAY, NOVEMBER 19—
AT HOME

That night, I fired up my laptop and sat with my back to the wall, facing the door in case Monique wandered in or my parents knocked. Now was not the time for anybody to look over my shoulder while I surfed.

For weeks, I'd made a point of trying *not* to find out about the so-called supplements Coach Kramer had been giving us. It was like I needed not to know. All of a sudden, I felt the opposite—like I couldn't go another night without the truth.

I didn't know the name of either the pills or the injections. I'd never seen the pill bottle, and Coach Kramer always wrapped his hand around the vial when he drew the liquid into the syringe. At least he used a different needle for each of us, so I didn't have to worry about catching a disease from one of my teammates. But would I have even said anything if he'd used the same needle on all of us? I hoped so. I didn't know, not for sure.

Anyhow, no way could I identify the injections without getting a look at that vial. But the little pink pills had a funny shape—five sides, a pentagon. I went online, typed in a quick image search, and bam. There they were. I was taking something called Dianabol.

I started scanning websites—official-looking ones from the government and medical clinics, plus bodybuilding sites. No surprise there: I got a different story depending on the source. The only thing all the sites agreed on was that without a doctor's prescription, Dianabol was illegal. The bodybuilding sites were pretty enthusiastic about careful, supervised steroid use. The medical sites, not so much.

I wondered if getting dosed by your football coach with no doctor's exam or tests counted as "careful, supervised use." Probably not.

What had I gotten myself into?

It was time to face the music. I took a look at the list of side effects on three medical sites. First up: acne, which made me remember that Ian was sporting quite the pizza face at practice that day. Well, fine. Who cares about a few zits if you're winning games?

Then the list turned serious. High cholesterol. High blood pressure. Possible cardiac arrest. Heart enlargement. Extreme mood swings—that must have been the "roid rage" Terry had exhibited. Stunted growth in teenagers. Liver malfunction. And on and on.

When I couldn't stand to read any more, I pulled out my phone. It was time to do one right thing for a change. I sent Curtis a text: *U around? Need to talk about that thing from the other night.*

The reply came within seconds: *Pick u up in 5.*

I didn't want to go to Doyle's—it wouldn't be good to run into anybody from the team. So I had Curtis drive to a Burger King on the other side of town. We snagged a couple of combo meals and sat for a few minutes, just eating.

"Look," I said finally. "What I'm gonna tell you has to stay here. You repeat it to no one, okay? *No one.*"

"Sure, man, you got it," Curtis replied.

"No matter what."

"What, you wanna pinky swear on it? Relax, Darius. This is me." I could see from the look in his eyes that he meant it. My best friend still had my back.

I took a deep breath and then told Curtis the whole thing. All of it. The pills, the injections, the results I'd had, the side effects I'd read about online. Finally, I told him I felt terrible about lying to him.

He listened intently, not saying a word till I was done. Then he gave a long, low whistle.

"You got some trouble here, D," he said.

"Tell me about it."

"Coach Kramer's got some guts, telling you guys to do this. It ain't right. It's dirty play."

"Yeah."

Curtis scowled. "Don't he think we're good enough to win on our own talent?"

I'd thought about that question myself. Truth was, I was pretty sure I wasn't good enough to get the starting slot on my own talent. Not without the juice. Maybe Coach Kramer felt that way about the team as a whole.

"I guess it's kind of like insurance," I said. "And he says the other teams are doing it too, so why shouldn't we?"

"And another thing." Curtis stabbed at the air with his finger. "Somebody's gonna get caught now that we're going to the playoffs. They test for this stuff, don't they?"

"Coach Kramer said not to worry about it. They pick random players to test, but they let you pee in the cup in your own locker room. So if any of us gets picked, Coach'll be ready with clean samples for us to use."

"Jeez," Curtis said. "The man's thought of everything, hasn't he?"

"Seems like it."

"You think Coach Z knows about it?"

I took a bite out of my burger before I answered. It tasted like cardboard. "I can't tell. I mean, he knows everything that goes on with the team, right? But then again, Coach Z has always played a clean game far as I know. It's kinda hard to believe he'd let this go on under his nose."

Curtis nodded. "Yeah, I bet you're right. I bet he agreed to let Coach Kramer set up the Elite Whatevers, and then Kramer started the juicing on his own." He slapped the table. "That's it, man. Coach Z can save the day here."

"How do you mean?"

"Tell him."

I felt my eyes practically pop out of my head. "Just like that? What if he already knows? He'll kick my butt off the team for betraying Coach Kramer."

"Naw, you don't tell him in person. E-mail him. You know, anonymously. He'll deal with it, he'll make Kramer stop, and nobody'll ever know it was you who spilled the beans."

Curtis was making sense. It was a better idea than anything I'd come up with, that was for sure.

"I'll think about it," I said. I felt something shift inside, like the weight in my stomach lifted for a few seconds. "Yeah," I said. "I will definitely think about that."

7/WEDNESDAY, NOVEMBER 20— TROY PUBLIC LIBRARY

It was one thing to think about playing narc, another to actually do it. I'd never ratted anybody out for anything. Then again, I'd never had any reason to. Probably the most illegal thing I'd ever seen was kids smoking pot at parties. I always figured, somebody wants to put that stuff in their body, who am I to care?

But now I was the one putting stuff in my body that didn't exactly belong there. And it was turning out that I cared a lot.

I chose the public library. The computer lab at school wasn't safe, and I didn't want to use my laptop. Paranoid? Probably. But if any kind of investigation ever came out of this, the last thing I'd need was my own computer incriminating me.

What I didn't know was that at the public library, they make you sign up for computer time with your library card. I gritted my teeth, decided that paranoia only made sense to a certain point, and got myself a seat at a PC. Seconds later, I'd created a Gmail account under a fake name.

I looked around to see if anybody was paying attention to me. Nope. A couple people were at terminals nearby, but they seemed to be engrossed in whatever they were doing. I started typing:

Coach Zachary,
Something dangerous to the team is going on. Check Coach Kramer's black gym bag.
                    A Concerned Fan

Okay, so it wasn't subtle. I didn't want it to be. Sure, Coach Z would see right through the "concerned fan" thing, but it seemed like a more strategic choice for my signature than *Wanna-Be Starting Halfback*.

"Darius!" A girl's voice rang out—it sounded a bit loud for the library, but that wasn't my worry. I clicked Send and minimized the browser window just as the voice's owner draped an arm around my shoulder. Charise Hawkins. Wow.

I tried to play it cool, like hot chicks singled me out every day instead of not at all. "Hey, girl, what up?"

Charise had the whole package: jaw-dropping curves, smooth skin, and a mind sharp enough to match all of it. She sat two seats in front of me in AP American Lit, and believe me, the girl knew her Fitzgerald from her Hemingway. I won't lie. I'd been crushing on her since seventh grade. But she was a junior, and I knew she wouldn't be caught dead with a tenth grader who didn't even have a driver's license. So I had never even tried.

Now here she was, acting like we were pretty close. The arm around my shoulder felt soft yet solid. Real, you know? She smelled good, like some kind of flower. Or a lot of kinds of flowers.

"What're you doin' here?" she said. "Working on that Faulkner paper?"

"Uh, yeah," I said. Wait, did that sound too geeky? "I mean, no—I mean, yes and no."

She gave me a sly little grin and raised her eyebrows.

"Gotta love a man who knows his own mind," she said.

I had to laugh. A girl like Charise probably had guys stammering and drooling all over themselves day in and day out. At least she didn't seem to be holding it against me.

"I would've thought you'd be, I dunno, lifting weights or something, not haunting the library." Her fingers played with my hair a little bit, casually, as if it was no big deal.

"Oh, there's no shortage of weight lifting in my life, believe me."

"You must be stressing out over the playoffs,

huh? You gonna carry us the way you did last Friday?" she said.

"That's the plan. You're gonna be there, right?" Relief. I'd finally found my big-boy voice.

"Oh, yeah. I don't wanna miss your next touchdown."

I gave her my best smile. "How 'bout I dedicate it to you, Miss Hawkins?"

Her eyes sparkled. I swear they were the deepest brown I've ever seen.

"You do that. I'll see you later, Red Hot Burns," she whispered in my ear.

That's when it hit me—when she called me Red Hot. Charise was no snob, but she'd never noticed me until I started to shine on the football field. Not that I blamed her. It's not exactly a surprise when a jock gets the girl, right?

But the thing was, the juice did it. The juice made her notice me. It wasn't me. At least not the real me. Knowing that somehow made the moment a little less sweet.

Still, I'd done what I came to do. I grabbed my backpack and dialed my dad on my phone. I needed a ride home.

8/THURSDAY, NOVEMBER 21—
TWO DAYS BEFORE PLAYOFFS

The next day, school whizzed right by. For the first time in weeks, I felt like I could really breathe. Pretty soon this whole thing would be over. Coach Kramer would be mad, sure, but if he wanted to keep his job, he'd have to do what Coach Z said. No more injections, no more pills. We could concentrate on tearing apart the Clinton Tigers in the playoffs and then cap it all off with a state championship.

Team practice was tough, just like it should be two days before the biggest game of the season so far. Between drills, I sneaked glances at Coach Kramer, looking for signs that he felt upset or anxious. But he chatted with Coach Z on the sidelines as usual, shouting out encouragement or criticism at whoever caught his eye.

I had another sharp day, handling the ball like I owned it, dancing around linemen and breaking tackles almost every play. I even blocked harder than normal, putting guys on the turf who would normally be wiping their cleats on me. As for Ian McNamara—well, let's just say that I had no worries about getting the start Friday night.

I figured Coach Kramer would hold his usual Elite Warriors practice after the team practice broke, and I was right. But I didn't expect it to end the way it did.

"Line up!" he yelled after our hour of drills. "Show me some hustle, men!"

On the locker room bench next to him sat the black gym bag where he kept the roids.

I blinked to clear my vision. Was I seeing

things? No, there was the vial. And he had the syringes out too.

Coach Z hadn't put a stop to it. I wondered if he had read my e-mail. Could it have gone into his spam folder? Or maybe he'd read it but hadn't had a chance to check Coach Kramer's gym bag?

"Burns," Coach Kramer said when my turn came up. "You're looking good out there, son. Keep it up. I know you're gonna shine come Saturday."

"Uh, yes, sir," I said. "I'll do my best."

"No, you won't," he answered. "You'll do better than your best." He flicked the tip of the syringe to clear out any air bubbles. "Sleeve up."

As I felt the needle go in, I thought about the other possibilities. Maybe Coach Z did read my e-mail. Maybe he hadn't looked in the gym bag because he already knew what was in there. Or maybe he had his suspicions but didn't want to find out for sure. Or maybe he looked, saw, and decided to play dumb to protect his own butt and increase our chances of winning state.

Keep your cool, Darius, I told myself. No

way to know yet. Give Coach Z another day.

And I did. But the next day was a rerun of the same scenario.

So much for Coach Z coming to the rescue. It was pretty clear now the position I was in. If anybody was going to keep me from juicing, it would have to be me.

9/SATURDAY, NOVEMBER 23—
STATE PLAYOFF GAME VS. CLINTON TIGERS

Since the Division I state playoffs and finals in Ohio are always played on Saturdays, and we didn't have too far to travel, we bused in from Troy that morning and watched the lower divisions play ahead of us. I won't lie. I was walking on the clouds. Coach Z told me the night before that the start would be mine, and judging from the look on Ian McNamara's face, he knew I was the man. All the work, all the extra time and sweat and sore muscles, all the stress—it would all pay off today. I could feel it.

We won the toss and elected to receive. Coach Z sent in Orlando Green, our star wide receiver, to bring back the kickoff. Orlando has a kind of speed I can only dream of—and, man, did he ever shine that day. He dodged and pivoted, got blocks in all the right places, and brought the ball back to our forty-five.

I lined up behind Shane as the crowd started to turn up the noise. These first couple plays were just blocks for me, opportunities for Shane to test Clinton's pass coverage. Nothing doing. Clinton's guys were all over Orlando, and Shane had to settle for connecting with Terry for a few yards on second down.

Third and five at midfield. My turn. I took the handoff from Shane and sprinted outside, pumping my legs like my life depended on it. A huge Tiger linebacker came at me. I dodged inside, then broke a tackle from my left. Orlando made a fantastic block for me—you gotta love a wide receiver who puts it on the line for a back.

And there it was, wide-open field stretched out like a long green ribbon in front of me. Two guys on my heels, but I left them wondering what had just happened. My cleats pounded the turf to the thirty... the twenty... No stopping me now. Yes! Trojans up, six–zero.

"Red Hot! Red Hot! Red Hot!" the crowd cheered. I pictured Charise up there among them, knowing this touchdown was just for her.

Everybody's got a different style when they score. I keep it mellow. None of that showboating in the end zone. I've seen guys do their little dances, pat themselves on the back, bow to the crowd. It's all about making themselves look good. I'd rather drop the ball and high-five my teammates. The glory is the same. The only difference is how much class you exhibit while you bask in the moment.

Seconds later, I punched through for the two-point conversion—Ian's signature play—and I wondered if he was cheering or fuming on the sidelines. Eight to zip.

From there, the game turned into a cake walk. The Tigers just didn't have it. They dropped passes, fumbled twice, and generally made themselves look more like a JV squad than a state championship contender. I scored again in the second quarter, and Orlando pulled in a touchdown as well. Score at halftime: Troy, twenty-four; Clinton, three.

In the locker room, Coach Z applauded us for kicking butt—then reminded us that a twenty-one-point lead can evaporate in minutes.

"Don't get arrogant," he said. "Don't think ahead. Get today's job done today."

As if to prove his point, Clinton put together an opening drive that led to a touchdown. But Shane answered a few plays later with a long, sweet pass to Orlando that put us up by twenty. Then I got my second score, a quick slant run from the five. Clinton managed another field goal, but we answered with a touchdown yet again to make it Troy, forty-five; Clinton, thirteen.

After that, it was all clock management. Clinton needed three touchdowns to win or even just to tie, and with nine minutes to go, their chances were lousy. Shane kept the ball on the ground, giving Dylan and Terry and me plenty of opportunities to carry. We ended up adding another TD plus two points along the way. Clinton was too rattled to respond—they never scored again after the third quarter.

We were in. We were going to state.

We were going to state!

10/SATURDAY, NOVEMBER 23—
AT HOME

I don't think I really knew what the word *bitter-sweet* meant until that moment. We were going to the finals—something I'd dreamed of doing since Coach Z's Half Backs youth camp. And it was happening in my sophomore year. Not only that, but I'd played a key part in getting us there. Yeah, this was some kind of sweetness.

But the bitter? Knowing I didn't do it on my own. Knowing *we* didn't do it on our own. I mean, come on, a big chunk of the offense was juicing! Even if some of the guys on the other teams were doing it too, like Coach Kramer was always saying, we'd never know whether our victories came out of our ability, our guts, and our desire—or a pill bottle and a syringe.

We'd never know if we would have won without the juice. Without cheating.

I couldn't fall asleep that night. When I finally drifted off, I dreamed about needles, dozens of discarded syringes with some kind of foul green liquid dripping from the tips. I woke with a jerk to find myself covered in sweat. It was three a.m.

I sat up in bed and turned on the light. Marion Motley gazed back at me from my desk. I wondered if they had the juice back in the 1940s and 1950s. Would Motley have taken it?

Something in my heart told me no.

The next day, we had team practice followed by Elite Warriors. No break on Sunday for a team that's going to state. When Coach Kramer called us to line up for our supplements—he'd switched us back to the pills again—I got in line like usual. But when my turn came, I looked him in the eye and cleared my throat.

"No, thank you, sir," I said.

"Whoa," one of the other guys said in a low voice—Terry, I think. And then there was silence.

"It's not optional, Burns," Coach said.

"No, thank you, sir," I repeated.

Coach Kramer got up in my face and stared me down. I'd never noticed how beady his eyes were. Beady and greenish, like a snake's.

"Son, let me just make sure that you understand the choice you're making here," he said. "You are on a conditioning program as a high-potential playmaker for this football team. You deviate from that program, there is no going back. You hear what I'm saying?"

"Yes, sir. I just don't think—"

"That's right. You don't think. I'm talking no more Elite Warriors. I'm talking no spot in the starting lineup at state. I say the word; Coach Z gives that slot to McNamara. And I will say the word." His face was turning redder with every syllable.

"I'd rather go back to second string than do something that's not right, sir."

"Second string? Second string?" he sputtered. "Burns, you will be *wishing* you could get back to second string if you leave this program. You'll be lucky if you get any minutes at state at all."

The longer I listened, the madder I got. Did Coach Kramer really think he had the right to keep me off the field for deciding not to juice?

He put his finger right in my face. I stepped back. He stepped forward.

"You want to talk about what's not right? Not right is you disregarding your obligation to this team, Burns. Not right is you claiming some glory while it's easy, then turning your back on your teammates and your coach when you start feel a little uncomfortable. Not right is—"

I'd heard enough. I turned around and walked away. I figured he'd keep yelling at me, but it was deadly quiet. As I made my way out of the locker room, he spoke one more time.

"McNamara," he said, keeping it loud. "You ready to see some action, son?"

I didn't have to wait to hear how that conversation turned out.

11/TUESDAY, NOVEMBER 26—
FOUR DAYS BEFORE STATE FINALS

I woke up feeling like somebody had taken an ice-cream scoop to the inside of my skull. And I was tired. Not football tired, not getting-sick tired, but a new kind of tired, something I'd never felt before. My whole body felt heavy, like my muscles just weren't interested in doing their job. Every step felt like walking through quicksand. Or molasses. Something thicker and stronger than I was.

All I wanted to do was go back to bed.

Maybe I was getting the flu, I thought. It was lousy timing. Not only did we have intensive practices all week to prep for state, I had a biology test that morning. And I had to be on my game academically if I wanted to keep my parents from putting me in tutoring.

I popped a couple of Advil on the way to school and reviewed my notes from class while Mama drove. She nodded approvingly.

"That's my son," she said. "Darius, I'm so proud of the way you're making school your top priority even though football's taking up so much of your time."

If only she knew. I'd fallen asleep at my desk the night before while studying for today's test. Even a B minus seemed out of reach, much less the kind of grade my parents expected.

Why is it that the hardest classes are always early in the day? No lunchtime or study hall to help me get ready. I'd just have to wing it.

Ms. Winthrop passed out the tests and

warned us to keep quiet, keep our eyes on our own paper, all the usual stuff. My headache felt worse than ever, and now I felt a stabbing pain in my gut too. I tried to focus on the words in front of me. Plants...yeah. *Photosynthesis*. Okay, I knew that one.

Stamen. Anther. Xylem. I was pretty sure the stamen was the skinny part in the middle of the flower, but otherwise, I was lost. It might as well have been Greek.

Come on, Darius! I rubbed my temples. You know this stuff. You studied. Well, you studied some. Remember? Come on, picture the textbook. Picture the words.

No good. I just needed to close my eyes for a minute. Let this headache pass.

Next thing I knew, somebody was ringing a cowbell right next to my ear. I opened my eyes, blinked a few times, and saw everybody around me passing their tests forward.

The cowbell wasn't a cowbell. It was the buzzer to signal the end of class.

I looked down at my paper. One definition filled in. The rest, blank. And a nice little puddle of drool right where I'd written my name.

I'd slept the entire period.

"Darius?" Ms. Winthrop stood over me, looking expectant.

"Um..." I scrambled for a strategy. "I'm feeling sick, Ms. Winthrop. Like, really sick." Actually, that wasn't a strategy. Just the truth.

She frowned. "I see. Well, let me write you a pass to the nurse. We'll discuss your exam later."

I let out my breath in a hiss. Biology tutor, here I come.

It wasn't until I was sitting in the nurse's office with a thermometer stuck in my mouth that I understood what might be happening to me. I pulled out my phone and searched "steroid withdrawal." There it was: fatigue, headache, nausea, abdominal pain...the list went on and on.

The best part? Going off steroids all at once, without tapering the dose, could be life-threatening.

Too bad Coach Kramer hadn't bothered to mention that. A flunked test was nothing. I'd be lucky if I didn't end up in the hospital.

12/WEDNESDAY, NOVEMBER 27—
LOCKER ROOM, BEFORE PRACTICE

It wasn't me who wound up in an ambulance, though.

The whole locker room was buzzing. Ian had gone down on the way to school that morning—just passed out right in the street. Paramedics revived him and took him to the hospital. Rumor was he had heart palpitations. Coach Z promised to keep us posted, but nobody could focus in practice that day.

It looked like I might be starting in state after all. Not that I wanted it to happen this way. I tried to imagine how Ian must be feeling. Was he scared? Angry? Did he feel like he was to blame for putting his parents through a world of hurt and worry?

The next day, Coach Z told us McNamara had improved. His doctor was keeping him in the hospital for observation, but he could have visitors.

Curtis drove me to see him after practice. "I'd come in with you," he said as he pulled up to the main entrance, "but hospitals give me the creeps."

"You and me both," I said. "Thanks for the ride, bro." We bumped fists, and I got out of the car.

Troy General Hospital must have been built in the 1970s, maybe earlier. It had a dated look, with ancient orange chairs in the waiting rooms and chipped tile floors underfoot. Even the walls looked tired, like nobody could pause long enough in the chaos of caring for patients to slap a fresh coat of paint over the dinginess.

I wandered among people in scrubs hurrying down corridors, visitors looking dazed and sometimes grieved, and the occasional patient being pushed in a wheelchair.

What was I doing here?

It wasn't that Ian was a friend, obviously. It wasn't even that he was a teammate, though that was part of it.

It was because of the juicing that I needed to see him. It was knowing that it could have been me lying in that hospital bed. Still could be, for that matter.

I found him on the sixth floor in a semiprivate room with an old man snoring in the other bed. He looked surprised to see me. His mom got up from the chair beside his bed and murmured something about going down to the cafeteria for dinner.

"Darius," he said, eyes narrowed. "Hadn't expected you to show up here."

"Hey, Ian." I put out my fist. He hesitated a moment, then pulled his hand out from under the covers and gave me a bump. A gadget was clipped to one of his fingers, with a cord leading to one of the machines beside the bed. A hospital bracelet wrapped around his wrist.

"Dude, you look hot in that gown." I cracked a grin, and McNamara laughed and told me to watch it. After that, talking to him got easier. I told him about practice, how everyone was asking about him and hoping he was okay.

"I can't believe I'm here," he said after a few minutes. "I mean, I'm fine now. I can't believe they're gonna keep my butt in this bed and make me miss state."

"Sucks, man," I said. "I guess you gave the docs a scare, huh."

"Well, I did pass out. So, yeah, everyone was pretty freaked out. But I'm fine now. It's just, you know, my parents want to be cautious, and the doctor says no way is he authorizing me to play football until I've had a few weeks with no further incidents." He rolled his eyes.

I tried to imagine what it would be like, losing the chance to start at state. Then I realized I already knew exactly what that was like.

I lowered my voice. "What happened to

you? Do they think it was because of—"

He cut me off. "Nobody knows about that. At least, not yet. But they're testing my blood for everything they can think of. So they'll know soon."

"What're you gonna do?"

"Nothing!" he said, scowling. "Not a thing. They can't make me tell them where I got it. No way am I gonna let them find out, either."

I had to admire his loyalty to Coach Kramer. I wondered what I'd do in the same position.

"Look," I said, "I read online about the side effects. They said you had heart palpitations, right?"

"Yeah."

"Well, it was probably the juice that did it. And it could have been a lot worse."

"What's your point, Burns? You think I should rat out Coach Kramer?"

I shook my head. "I just hope you'll turn him down if he wants you to keep doing it. That's all."

Ian exploded. "You don't get it, do you? You aren't gonna have to worry about me juicing,

Burns, because once that blood test comes back, I'm through. It'll get reported to the state athletic board, and they'll ban me. Probably for good."

It took me a minute to process his words. Banned from football? For good? But it wasn't Ian's fault, not really. We were all under a lot of pressure from a guy who held a ton of power over us. A guy we should've been able to trust.

"I'm sorry, man." I tried to look him in the eye, but he turned toward the guy in the next bed, who had kept snoring through the yelling.

"Whatever. Enjoy starting at state."

"I—"

"In my spot. Which, by the way, I earned. You quit the Elite. I stuck with them, and I earned the start. Now it's all for nothing."

I just stood there. He was wrong—the starting spot was rightfully mine. Wasn't it? Besides, I had good reasons for quitting the juice when I did. It was only the twisted logic of Coach Kramer that said I'd taken the easy way out.

This was no time to argue ethics, though.

"Just feel better, Ian," I said. "Take care."

I didn't wait for another blowup, just turned and left the room. The headache I'd been fighting all day throbbed inside my skull. What had I been thinking, coming to see Ian? Of course he was angry at me. I would be too in his position.

Suddenly, all I wanted was to get out of that stupid hospital. I rounded a corner too quickly and smacked into a big guy.

"Watch it!" he barked.

"Sorry," I mumbled. Then I realized who I was talking to. It was Coach Kramer.

We locked eyes for a minute.

"No worries, Coach," I said in a low voice dripping with sarcasm. "He's not gonna give anything away. Your secret is safe."

His beady green eyes narrowed. "You watch your mouth, Burns."

"Oh, sorry," I said. And then, because I knew he could cause me plenty of trouble with Coach Z, I added, "Sir."

"Out of my way."

I'd made my point. I stepped aside and stared as my coach's back as he went to visit the guy he'd put in the hospital.

13/SATURDAY, NOVEMBER 30— STATE CHAMPIONSHIP GAME DAY

The state championship game for our division takes place in Canton, home of the Pro Football Hall of Fame and Fawcett Stadium. We bused in the day before—the whole team got the day off school, along with the cheerleaders—and spent the night in a hotel.

A bunch of the guys went out for pizza with the coaches, followed by a swim party with the girls at the hotel's indoor pool, but I begged off. All I wanted to do was sleep.

And then it was game day. It all came down to this. We'd go home tonight as champs or losers, no in-betweens.

In the morning, we held a short practice to get a feel for the stadium and the field. Nothing too strenuous, though I think Coach could've had us run suicides and still had a team that was ready for more punishment against the Athens High Raiders.

The guys were seriously pumped. Athens, the Evil Empire, has been Troy Central High's biggest rival for as long as the two programs have existed. Most of the guys were pumped, that is. I put on a good show, but between my pounding head and the feeling that my blood had somehow been replaced with cement, I was dragging big time.

Back in the locker room, Coach Z read off four names and passed out plastic cups for the so-called random drug testing. None of the four were Elite Warriors. Or ex-Elite Warriors, for that matter. I wondered if Coach Kramer was pulling the strings behind the scenes somehow. But at least I had nothing to worry about.

After lunch, we rode in the Trojans team bus to the Pro Football Hall of Fame for a tour. I'd been there before, but they add new stuff every year. Highlights from every Super Bowl on a twenty-foot screen, an interactive "you make the call" play booth, that kind of thing. Very cool.

When I asked one of the guides about Marion Motley, he got pretty excited. Turned out they had his 1946 contract with the Cleveland Browns right there in the museum, and the guide got it out of the archives to show us. Motley made four thousand bucks that season, which the guide said would be about fifty grand today. Decent money back then. I stared at his signature and tried to imagine how it must have felt to get paid to do something he loved so much. Not many people get to live that kind of life, you know?

After the Hall of Fame, we got a couple hours of free time. You guessed it; I took a nap in the hotel. Then came a light, early dinner.

Finally, we bused back to Fawcett Stadium. It was time to suit up.

My head wouldn't let up no matter how much I slept. I swallowed four Advils just before I slid my helmet on.

I'd been here before as a spectator, watching last year's championship game, so I thought I knew what to expect when we ran out of the tunnel. But the perspective from the field is nothing like it is up in the stands. I'd never been surrounded by twenty thousand screaming fans before, never anything close to that many. Even in the open-air stadium, the noise was crushing. I wondered if it was physically possible for someone's head to pop off from steroid withdrawal.

Somewhere in that ocean of people sat my mom and dad and Monique. Charise too. I hoped I would do them proud.

Athens won the coin toss and elected to receive, so it was a while before I got out on the field. By then, we were down a TD and the Athens fans were going nuts. I kept shaking my head, trying to clear the pain and clear my thoughts too. This was the most important game of my life, yet I couldn't focus. Couldn't even feel the intensity, though I knew it was all around me. It was like someone had dropped a curtain between me and the rest of the world.

Still, I had a job to do. I took my handoffs and ran as hard as I could. But I couldn't make much headway. Shane picked up on it right away, and pretty soon he was hitting Orlando and the other receivers instead of giving me the ball. But all of us seemed off during those first couple of drives.

Athens took advantage. Ten minutes into the game, we found ourselves down fourteen–zero.

Coach Z called timeout and read us the riot act.

"You guys are better than this!" he roared. "You are better than they are! You have the speed, the agility, the guts. What you don't seem to have is the desire. Do you want this or not?"

"Yeah!" everyone yelled.

"Then get out there and prove it to me!"

And just like that, everyone stepped up. Curtis intercepted the very next pass to set us up for a quick touchdown. Shane fired a short pass to Orlando for the two-point conversion. On their next possession, Athens went three-and-out. We followed with a field goal, then another to tie it up at fourteen. And then Athens fumbled, giving us the ball at midfield.

Shane pulled us together in the huddle and called a reverse play. It was a no-brainer. A quick handoff to me, a lateral run just behind the line of scrimmage, and a handoff to Terry. We lined up, and Shane took the snap. I snagged the handoff—no problem—and sprinted to the left.

But something went wrong. Terry wasn't where he was supposed to be. Neither was my blocker. In fact, the only guy there was a six-foot-tall Raider who proceeded to pummel me into the turf.

I popped back up like it was nothing and joined the huddle, only to find myself face-to-face with a very angry QB1.

"Wrong direction! Burns!" he sputtered.

I just stared at him. "No, Terry wasn't there—"

"Oh, I was there," Terry cut in. "You ran the wrong freaking way, Darius. We're lucky Athens didn't let you keep going."

That's when I realized what I'd done. It was worse than a rookie mistake. It was the kind of mistake a guy makes when his head's not in the game. And mine sure wasn't. It was too busy trying not to implode.

So much for momentum. With the help of the down I wasted, we went three-and-out. Midway through the second quarter, Athens took it in for another TD. That left us down by seven.

I'd only had a couple of touches since my screwup, and I hadn't done anything spectacular with them. Finally, as the half wound down, Shane lit up Orlando in the end zone. Orlando pulled the ball in like he owned it. Now we were down just a point.

Coach Z could've gone for the kick and the sure tie going into halftime, but that's never been his way. He called for a two-point conversion.

I'd be carrying the ball. You can do this, I told myself as we lined up. You got this, Darius.

"Hut! Hut! Hut!" Shane yelled. Helmets, pads, and bodies collided. I took the handoff, pulled the ball in close, and stuck my left arm out to block. Ahead of me, Dylan smashed into a lineman. Sure enough, a hole opened. I pushed ahead, but the hole started narrowing fast. I needed more speed than I could coax out of my muscles.

Smash! I rammed into a Raider, then another, and then a third came at me from the side. I hit the turf, still cradling the ball, but I knew I was way short of the goal line.

The ref blew the whistle. The silence from Troy's side of the bleachers confirmed my failure. As I lay flattened at the bottom of the pile, guys slowly picked themselves up, and the horn blew to signal the end of the half. When I could see again, I didn't even have to look, but of course I did anyway. A full yard short.

Dylan pulled me up, and a couple guys gave me a friendly slap as we jogged into the tunnel.

All I got from Shane was a glare. He hurried ahead to talk to Coach Z, and I knew what was coming.

The worst part was that I was almost glad.

14/STATE CHAMPIONSHIP GAME— HALFTIME

I'd never been in such a quiet locker room. My teammates barely even breathed as Coach Z rattled off a list of our faults: sloppy special teams work, lousy defensive blocking, the dropped interception. And then he got to me.

"Burns, what is going on with you? Are you even awake out there? What was that botched reverse?"

"I'm sorry, sir," I said.

"Well, I'm sorry too, son, but your teammates are out there getting pounded, and you can't tell your right from your left? And how many times have you made that blast for two points this season? Only to miss it when it counts the most?"

I had a feeling he didn't really intend me to answer any of those questions, so I kept my mouth shut. He wasn't done with me yet, though.

"You've got your own QB1 asking me to bench you, you know that?" Coach Z sputtered. "And I'm of a mind to do exactly that. We'll see if Vasquez can make a play when it counts."

Miguel Vasquez was the backup's backup, the guy who began the season expecting zero minutes because Devon, Ian, and I were all in his way. And now he was taking my place in the state championship. Congratulations, Darius. Your humiliation is complete.

I tried to stay focused on the rest of Coach Z's lecture, just in case he changed his mind and put me back in after all, but the headache I was sure couldn't get worse had started thundering inside my skull again. It was all I could do to keep my eyes open and look like I was paying attention. I didn't have it in me to actually listen, much less process what I heard.

A few minutes later, we jogged back out of the tunnel to face our rival and our fate. Our guys definitely took Coach Z's words to heart. The second half opened with Orlando Green running back the kickoff ninety yards for a sweet six points—and then my backup iced the cake by punching through for the two-point conversion. I cheered Vasquez on as loud as anybody. Score: Troy, twenty-eight; Athens, twenty-one.

The rest of the third quarter was a see-saw of scoring: them, us, them, us. Both defenses looked ragged. Curtis made some sweet tackles, though, forcing the Raiders to settle for a field goal on one play and causing a fumble on another.

As the fourth quarter began, it was Troy, thirty-nine; Athens, thirty-one. Not a lot of breathing room, and the coaches looked tenser than I'd ever seen them. Shane made it worse a few minutes in by throwing a rare interception. At least Dylan brought the guy down at the Athens ten, so they had a long way to go. But the Raiders put together a fierce drive, eating up the clock and plowing through our defensive line a few yards at a time. They scored on the fourteenth play of the drive. They followed the touchdown with another two points to tie it up with four minutes and change left to play.

I knew I wasn't the only one thinking about my botched two-point conversion. It had made the difference so far. Would my team rise above my mistakes?

I have to admit, I was worried that Shane wouldn't be able to shake off that interception. I shouldn't have been concerned. He may be a jerk, but he's a jerk with the most intense focus I've ever seen on the football field. He hit Orlando for two passes in a row, then mixed it up with a pitch to Dylan that gained us sixteen yards.

Next, the Trojan offense ran the reverse

play—the same one I'd botched in the first quarter, only this time Vasquez executed perfectly. Shane ran it in himself for the touchdown, then did the exact same thing for the two. Athens didn't know what had hit them.

With a minute-ten remaining, the Raiders tried to put something together, but they were out of time-outs and they quickly ran out of time. They'd only made it to midfield when Curtis pulled down the last tackle of the game. Final score: Troy, forty-seven; Athens, thirty-nine.

We did it. We won state. I'd had the worst game of my career. I'd been benched in the most embarrassing way possible, but my boys had taken the prize. And I was as much a part of the celebration as anybody, giving Coach Z a Gatorade shower, whooping it up in the locker room, and finally forgetting that evil headache for a few minutes.

I didn't forget that we got there by cheating, though. But a bunch of those guys—in fact, most of them—had played by the book, and they deserved every minute of bliss. They had earned it. I gave Vasquez a high five and complimented his game. He looked like a little kid in a candy store, all wide-eyed and full of joy.

Next thing we knew, we were piled on the team bus for the trip home. And the season was suddenly over.

15/MONDAY, DECEMBER 2—
TEAM MEETING

Two days after winning state, you'd think a football coach would be pumping the guys up, getting us revved for off-season workouts. Not this time.

"Gentlemen," Coach Z began, his face stern. "We have a serious situation on this football team. As you know, Ian McNamara was hospitalized last week due to heart palpitations. It's since come to light that he was taking anabolic steroids, which were the likely cause of his health issues."

The guys started talking all at once—except the Elite Warriors. Most of them looked at the floor, at the ceiling, anywhere but at each other or Coach Kramer.

"Enough!" Coach Z yelled.

Everyone shut up.

"I know I don't have to tell you that those substances are illegal and absolutely contrary to the values this school and this team stand for. Not to mention dangerous. Now, as far as we know, McNamara's actions were known to him alone. But the state athletic board will be investigating. If they find that anyone who played on Saturday—or in any of our prior games—was doping, our victory will be vacated. We will no longer be state champions."

I'd never seen such a grim bunch of guys. Coach Z might as well have said that Ian had died. In fact, I had a nasty suspicion that some of my teammates would have rather heard that than Coach Z's actual words.

"I expect that every one of you will cooperate

fully with the investigation. Do the right thing for yourself, your team, and your school. If anyone has any questions, see me individually."

Coach scanned the room, looking at each of us in turn. Maybe my mind was playing tricks on me, but I could swear he let his gaze linger a beat longer on each of the Elite Warriors.

How much did he know? And what did he really mean about doing the right thing for the team?

Walking home from practice, I tried to figure it out. Telling the truth would mean humiliation for the school, the team, even my family. It would mean no more football for me, no college scholarship, maybe no college at all. At least not Princeton like my parents wanted. There'd probably be a suspension from school and that would go on my record and . . .

Plus Coach Kramer would lose his job. Maybe Coach Z too.

Actually, I almost could live with that. Kramer had rolled the dice with our health and safety for the sake of winning. And if Coach Z didn't know about it—which I doubted—he should've. He should've been looking out for us.

Still, did I want to be the guy who single-handedly destroyed the Trojan football legacy? Destroyed careers, destroyed everybody's chances to play college ball?

On the other hand, telling would mean I wouldn't have to live with being a cheater. I wouldn't have to live with covering up the truth about how Ian ended up in the hospital. Why should he take the blame for something his coach pushed him into doing?

It was too much. I had to stop thinking about it for a while. I called Curtis to see if he wanted to come over for a *Call of Duty* marathon. An hour later, we were blasting our way through enemy defenses, lobbing grenades, and generally kicking butt.

Would I tell the truth? I'd have to wait and see.

16/MONDAY, DECEMBER 9—
TEAM MEETING

I didn't have to wait long. The investigation turned out to be a joke. Nobody even contacted me. No questions to answer, no tough choices to make.

Well, I could've chosen to come forward with what I knew. But I didn't.

Coach Z was grinning like the cat that ate the canary when he gave us the news.

"I'm pleased to tell you all that the state

athletic board has concluded that Ian McNamara acted alone in his use of banned substances," he said. "No evidence was found that any other Trojan broke any regulation."

It's never a good idea to interrupt Coach Z, but I guess Shane couldn't help himself. "So the state championship stands?"

Coach Z shot him a look, but he couldn't keep the smile off his face for long. "Correct. Since McNamara didn't play in the championship, and no proof was found that he was using steroids when he played in previous games, all our victories remain on the books. Congratulations, gentlemen. We are state champions!"

With that, all the tension that had gripped us since Ian went into the hospital seemed to evaporate. Curtis jumped up and gave me a high five, which set everybody off into about five minutes of whooping, hollering, and cheering. As the noise died down, Dylan raised his hand. Coach Z gave him a nod.

"Where's Coach Kramer, sir?"

Everybody looked around. All the assistants were in their usual spots except him.

Coach Z cleared his throat. "Coach Kramer had to attend to a family situation. He'll continue to teach, but because he needs more time at home right now, he'll be on leave from coaching through the off-season. Possibly beyond."

I could have sworn Coach Z caught my eye right then—just like he had the week before—and gave me the smallest of all possible nods.

17/TUESDAY, DECEMBER 17— PRACTICE FIELD

It took another week off the juice to start feeling like myself again. I made myself run a couple miles every day. Plus my parents kept their promise to get me a biology tutor, so I had plenty of things to occupy my time while the headache faded. To top it all off, Ms. Winthrop decided I could do an extra credit project since I'd been "sick" the day of the test I flunked. One more thing I'd be keeping quiet about, probably for the rest of my life.

Most of the guys had taken a couple weeks off working out after state. Nobody could hold an organized practice, of course, but we had our instructions for strength training and conditioning. That's why Curtis and I were on the field after school, timing each other on the forty-yard dash.

No surprises there. My times sucked. I had a lot of work to do, a lot of things to make up for.

"Well, look who's putting in some overtime."

I turned around. It was Charise Hawkins, standing on the sideline. I wondered how long she'd been watching us run.

"Yo, Curtis, gimme a few minutes," I called out. My buddy took the hint, waved, and jogged off to run a lap around the sidelines.

Suddenly I had no idea what to say. Charise hadn't even talked to me since state. I figured I'd blown whatever chance I might've had with her, playing like I did. So what was she doing here now?

"Uh, what's up, Charise?"

"Not much. Just taking a shortcut home from play rehearsal." I remembered she had a part in *Oklahoma!*—yeah, on top of everything else, the girl could sing.

"Oh." I tried to think of something intelligent to say about the musical, but as usual, my tongue was tied in a double knot.

"You've been pretty quiet lately, Darius," she said.

"I have?"

"Mm-hmm. I don't think you've said three words to me since football season ended."

"Huh?"

"It's true." She didn't sound annoyed. Just curious.

"Um, well . . . I mean, you were really nice to me for a while, but then I had a rough night at state, so I figured . . ." I wondered if it was possible to set a record in awkwardness with the female of the species. If so, I surely had a good start at it.

"You thought I was being nice to you because of *football*?" She looked at me like I had two heads but no brains.

"Well—I mean—you called me Red Hot, like everybody else was doing, but then—"

I have perfected the art of the stammer. Truly I have.

Charise crossed her arms and raised her eyebrows. "But then you played like crap at state, so now I must not like you?"

"Wow. You don't mince words, do you?"

"I call it like I see it." She smiled, like she was up to something. And then she waited.

I had to take a chance. "Well, you know I'd love to ask you out, but—"

"But what?"

"But I'm a sophomore, I don't have my license yet, and I don't think having my mom drop us off at the movies sounds too romantic, know what I mean?"

She raised her eyebrows again. "You don't have a driver's license?"

"Nope."

"Well, so what? I do." And then she leaned in to whisper in my ear. "Maybe football gave me an excuse to talk to you, Darius, but it's not the *reason* I wanted to talk to you. Get it?"

Her breath smelled like cinnamon. I nodded. "Yeah, I think I do."

"All right then. I'd say the ball's in your court, but that would be the wrong sport, wouldn't it?" She gave me that mischievous little smile again.

"So how 'bout I call you tonight?" I said.

She recited her number, which I memorized like it was the meaning of life itself. Then she walked off the field, leaving me in quiet shock.

Curtis jogged up before I had a chance to recover my cool. "Is it just me, or is that girl into you?"

"It's not just you."

He gave me his usual punch in the shoulder. "Darius, my man! Makin' time with the ladies!"

I just laughed. "Clock me for a few more?"

"Sure."

Maybe, after the ups and downs of this messed-up season, I could make a new beginning. Maybe I could rise above the choices I regretted and earn that starting spot on next year's team the old-fashioned way.

Or maybe I'd end up playing another year as backup. Devon would be back with his wrist healed, ready to fight for his position. But I've never been afraid to compete.

When Curtis yelled "Go!" I launched myself into a sprint.

When you run the forty, you can't tell how fast you're going. But I could tell one thing: My natural strength, my natural speed, were coming back to me. I ran with a lightness I hadn't felt all season.

ABOUT THE AUTHOR

Shannon Knudsen grew up watching St. Louis Cardinals football. These days, she lives in Arizona, so the Cardinals are still high on her list. But her real passion is the Minnesota Vikings. She says it's not always easy being a Vikings fan, but she's confident that someday her loyalty will pay off. When it's not football season, she spends her free time watching college basketball, playing video games, and walking her two dogs.

WINNING IS *NOT OPTIONAL.*

OUT OF THE TUNNEL

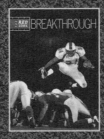

BREAKTHROUGH

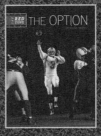

THE OPTION

AT ALL COSTS

TAKE AWAY

RISE ABOVE

LOOK FOR THESE TITLES FROM THE

TRAVEL TEAM

COLLECTION.

WELCOME TO

THE DOJO

BODY SHOT
PATRICK JONES

HEAD KICK
PATRICK JONES

LEARN TO FIGHT, LEARN TO LIVE, AND LEARN TO FIGHT FOR YOUR LIFE.

SIDE CONTROL
PATRICK JONES

TRIANGLE CHOKE
PATRICK JONES